Operation Baby-Sitter

Matt Christopher

Text by Stephanie Peters

Illustrated by Daniel Vasconcellos

Little, Brown and Company
Boston New York London

To Duane, Karen, and Michelle

First Paperback Edition

Library of Congress Cataloging-in-Publication Data

Peters, Stephanie.
Operation baby-sitter / by Stephanie Peters ; illustrated by Daniel Vasconcellos. — 1st ed.
p. cm. — (The Soccer Cats ; #2)
Summary: Ten-year-old Bundy finds his performance and attitude as captain of his soccer team suffering when he is saddled with a baby-sitter at home.
ISBN 0-316-13723-5 (hc)/0-316-13556-9 (pb)
[1. Soccer — Fiction. 2. Baby-sitters — Fiction.]
I. Vasconcellos, Daniel, ill. II. Title. III. Series: Christopher, Matt. Soccer Cats ; #2.
PZ7.C4580p 1999
[Fic] — dc21 98-42430

HC: 10 9 8 7 6 5 4 3 2
PB: 10 9 8 7 6 5 4 3 2

WOR

COM-MO

Printed in the United States of America

Soccer 'Cats Team Roster

Lou Barnes	*Striker*
Jerry Dinh	*Striker*
Stookie Norris	*Striker*
Dewey London	*Halfback*
Bundy Neel	*Halfback*
Amanda Caler	*Halfback*
Brant Davis	*Fullback*
Lisa Gaddy	*Fullback*
Ted Gaddy	*Fullback*
Alan Minter	*Fullback*
Bucky Pinter	*Goalie*

Subs:

Jason Shearer

Dale Tuget

Roy Boswick

Edith "Eddie" Sweeny

Chapter 1

"Bundy! Take it!"

Halfback Bundy Neel, his dark hair sticking straight up, raced to the open spot. He stopped Dewey's pass, then dribbled the ball toward the Panthers' goal.

It was the Soccer 'Cats' second game of the summer. It was midway through the second half. The score was tied, 4–4.

Bundy was team captain and wanted to help his squad to a victory. When he had been voted in as team captain, he'd been excited and a little surprised. He had been sure his pal Dewey London was going to be named captain. After all, Dewey had won the team's logo-design contest. According to the rules of the contest, the winner was supposed to become team captain automatically.

But Dewey didn't want to be captain. He had stood in front of the whole team and nominated Bundy for that job. The whole team had seconded the nomination.

After the vote, the coach had asked Bundy to stick around. "That was a nice move on Dewey's part, don't you think?" he had said to Bundy.

Bundy nodded.

"It's that sort of behavior I want my team captain to have," Coach Bradley continued. "In my book, the best kind of leader leads by example. When the other kids see you giving extra effort, or going for the assist instead of the goal, or just being a good sport even if the team's having an off day, they'll do the same things. Right?"

"Right!" Bundy had agreed.

So during the week's practices, Bundy had run faster, worked harder, and shown even more enthusiasm for the game than he usually did. He hadn't been sure, but he thought his teammates were starting to give more, too.

Now Bundy dribbled the ball just across the center line. Two Panthers swept in on either side. A third charged him from the front.

Stookie Norris, a striker, called to Bundy. If anybody could break the tie, it was Stookie.

Bundy pulled his foot back to kick a pass. Out of the corner of his eye, he saw the attacker on his right move in. He tried to protect the ball, but the Panther stole it anyway.

Bundy raced after him. In a second, he was running beside him. He knew what he had to do—tackle from the side. It was a tricky move. He had to make sure he was a little ahead of his opponent so he wasn't attacking from behind. Attacking from behind was a serious foul. He also had to be careful not to kick his opponent. That's where Bundy usually messed up.

And it's where he messed up this time, too. He positioned his body perfectly. But when his foot snaked in to snare the ball, he whacked the Panther's shin.

Pheet! The ref blew his whistle and pointed a finger at Bundy.

"Direct kick!" he said, tossing the ball to the Panther.

Bundy danced around, trying to guess who would receive the kick. A tall, thin Panther darted forward. Bundy lunged toward him, but he was too late. The kicked ball was stopped by the thin Panther's foot.

The Panther dribbled the ball a few feet toward the 'Cats' goal. Then he booted it upfield. The kick looked strong, but the ball stopped before reaching a teammate.

Bundy rushed to get it. He pulled up short when he saw Dewey, the center midfielder,

PANTH

intercept it. *Now* the ball was headed in the right direction!

"Dewey! Over here!" Bundy yelled, racing toward the Panther goal.

Dewey sent him the ball. Bundy gave it a solid boot toward the Panthers' net. The ball soared high over the heads of Panthers and 'Cats alike. Then it soared over the goal and bounced behind the goal line.

Chapter 2

Bundy, why didn't you pass to me?" an angry voice beside him said. It was Stookie. "I was in perfect position."

"You were?" Bundy groaned. "Man, I really blew it."

Stookie sighed heavily. "No, that's okay. You would have passed it to me if you'd seen me. I know you're not a ball hog." He punched Bundy lightly in the shoulder. "If you were, do you think we would have let you be captain?"

Bundy shot Stookie a grateful smile and

hurried to his spot. Stookie's comment made missing the goal a little easier.

And next time, he promised himself, *I'll look for the pass before I go for the goal!*

The game continued. Bundy was taken out, and Edith "Eddie" Sweeny subbed in. Bundy didn't mind. He knew Coach Bradley always gave every player a chance on the field.

Eddie attacked her opponents with gusto. But she couldn't seem to get the ball to any of her teammates. After five minutes, Coach Bradley had Bundy sub back in.

As Bundy passed a disappointed Eddie, he said, "You really scared the pants off some of those Panthers, Eddie." Eddie grinned and continued to the bench looking a little happier.

It was the Panthers' out. In seconds, the inbounded ball was headed straight into 'Cats territory. Bundy pounded after it.

But the Panthers were quick. Their striker dodged around fullbacks Brant Davis and

Lisa Gaddy. Ted, Lisa's twin brother, collided with Alan Minter. The Panther walloped a kick toward the far corner of the net. Goalie Bucky Pinter hurled himself after it. He missed it by inches.

Now the score was Panthers 5, 'Cats 4. There was only a minute left to play.

"Come on, let's tie it up!" Bundy called. "It ain't over till it's over!"

But when the horn blared, signaling the end of the game, the score was still the same. The 'Cats walked off the field with their heads down.

Bundy did his best to rally them. "We played a good game, 'Cats," he said over and over. "And we'll get 'em next time."

After collecting their stuff, Dewey and Bundy walked home together as usual. They talked over the game, then parted to go to their own houses.

When Bundy turned into his driveway, he was surprised and happy to see his grandfather's car. Surprised because Grandpa Frederic had been on vacation for the last week. Happy because Bundy loved spending time with his grandfather. Both of Bundy's parents worked, so it was Grandpa Frederic who welcomed Bundy home after school during the school year and who stayed with Bundy during the summer weekdays.

Bundy's parents were with his grandfather in the kitchen. They all looked serious.

Uh-oh, Bundy thought. *I wonder what's going on.*

Chapter 3

He didn't have long to find out.

"Grandpa Frederic has something to tell you, Bundy," Mrs. Neel said. Her voice sounded a little funny.

Grandpa Frederic cleared his throat. "You know I was in Florida last week, right?"

Bundy nodded.

"Well, I found a nice house when I was there."

"A house?" Bundy echoed. "What for?"

Grandpa Frederic chuckled. "What are houses usually for?" He turned serious.

"Bundy, I've decided to move to Florida. Snowy winters aren't much fun for me anymore."

Bundy's mouth sagged. Grandpa Frederic was *moving?*

Grandpa Frederic smiled gently. "Come on, look on the bright side. You can come visit me, and we'll go to all those cool amusement parks together." He scratched his chin. "I might even get on a roller coaster."

"Dad!" Mrs. Neel scolded, laughing. Then she turned to Bundy and dropped the second bombshell of the day.

"Since your grandpa is moving," Mrs. Neel said, "your dad and I have hired a girl to come over every day. She'll have a car, so she can take you wherever you need to go and—"

"Wait a minute," Bundy interrupted, a look of horror on his face. "Are you saying I'm going to have a—a—*baby-sitter?*"

Mr. and Mrs. Neel exchanged a glance.

"Now, Bundy, don't make it sound so bad,"

Mrs. Neel said. "You and Mary have a lot in common. In fact, she—"

"But I'm ten years old!" Bundy cried. "I can take care of myself."

Mr. Neel looked pained. "Your mother and I aren't comfortable with that, Bundy."

His grandfather laid a hand on his arm. "Bundy," he said gently, "what's so wrong with having someone look after you? That's all I ever did."

Bundy shook his head. "It was different with you. My friends all thought it was cool that we hung out together. But if the other 'Cats find out I have to have a *baby-sitter*—" The rest of the thought was too terrible to say out loud. He shoved his chair away from the table and ran up the stairs to his bedroom.

Hot tears pricked his eyes as he flung himself onto his bed.

A baby-sitter, he thought disgustedly. *The captain of a soccer team can't have a baby-sitter.*

He rolled over and stared at the ceiling.

There's only one thing to do, he decided. *I'll have to make her quit. In the meantime, I'll have to make sure none of the 'Cats finds out about her!*

Chapter 4

Grandpa Frederic left for Florida a few days later. He gave Bundy a big hug in the airport.

"Give the baby-sitter a chance," he whispered. Bundy didn't say anything. He just held on to his grandpa with all his might.

Then Grandpa Frederic was gone. Bundy watched the plane until it was a dot in the sky.

It was Friday. The baby-sitter wouldn't start until after the weekend. He had three days to come up with a plan.

At practice, his mind was in a jumble. Part of it was missing his grandfather. Another part was thinking about the baby-sitter. Still another part was trying to figure out what to do about her.

And underneath all these parts was a tiny section that whispered Grandpa Frederic's last words to him: *Give the baby-sitter a chance.*

He pushed the whisper away and tried to concentrate on practice.

The coach blew his whistle and called the team together.

"We're going to work on defensive moves today," Coach Bradley said. "Bundy, since you seem to be having a little trouble with the block tackle from the side, I'm going to have you focus on that. Eddie, pair off with him. Now, the rest of you . . ."

Eddie Sweeney jumped up, dropped a ball at her feet, and started dribbling down the field.

Bundy chased after her. He rushed up on her right side and got his left foot in close to the ball. He spun into tackle position. Quick as a wink, he made the steal!

"Okay, that's better," Coach Bradley praised him. He had sent other pairs of players to practice different moves, then returned to where Bundy and Eddie were playing. "Now try it again."

This time, Eddie was better prepared, so Bundy had a little more difficulty. But he finally stole the ball.

For the next ten minutes, Bundy worked on the tackle. Sometimes he was successful. But a lot of times Eddie made it down the length of the field with the ball.

Finally, he and Eddie switched positions. Her red hair blazing in the sun, Eddie looked determined to master the tackle.

She didn't have to work very hard. Coach Bradley was on the other side of the field, and Bundy's mind was on his baby-sitter problem again. After a few halfhearted plays,

Eddie put her hands on her hips and glared at him.

"What?" Bundy said stupidly.

Eddie rolled her eyes. "What will it take to make you pay attention?" She got a gleam in her eye. "Oh, wait—I have an idea." She suddenly stomped on Bundy's left foot.

"Ow!" he yelped. "What'd you do that for?"

Eddie smiled sweetly. "I don't like to be ignored."

Bundy stared at her. A thoughtful look crossed his face. "Being ignored makes you angry, huh? Hmm." He started to smile. "Eddie, you just gave me a great idea! I could kiss you for it."

Eddie backed off. "Don't even think about it, Bundy Neel," she warned. "Or your right foot will feel like your left one!"

Chapter 5

When Monday morning arrived, Bundy had Operation Baby-Sitter all figured out. He almost couldn't wait for his parents to leave so he could put it to the test.

Bundy answered the doorbell when it rang.

Mary was a tall, athletic-looking girl. She wore gym shorts and a T-shirt with a sports design on it. Her long black hair was pulled back into a ponytail, her bangs falling just above her eyes. She carried a big duffel bag.

"So, you're Bundy, huh?" Bundy just

shrugged and motioned for her to follow him into the kitchen.

Bundy was stone-faced at the kitchen table. His parents chattered to fill the silence.

"Bundy's got his soccer game this afternoon," Mrs. Neel said, "but his morning is free. So you should have plenty of time to get to know each other. Right, Bundy?"

Bundy didn't answer.

Mr. Neel pointed out the emergency phone numbers on the fridge. "Not that we expect Bundy to eat poison or anything. At least, not on your first day, ha, ha," he joked lamely. Mary smiled and shot Bundy a quick "parents-can-be-so-silly" look.

But Bundy just looked down.

Finally, his parents left.

Okay, Bundy thought as he closed the door behind them, *time for Operation Baby-Sitter to go into effect!*

He turned from the door and walked across the kitchen.

"So, what do you feel like doing?" Mary said, reaching for her duffel bag. "Your folks told me you play . . ."

Her voice trailed away as Bundy walked up the stairs to his bedroom. Bundy could feel her eyes on him the whole way. Only when he shut the bedroom door did he let out the breath he'd been holding.

Ignoring Mary was harder than he'd thought. But he was sure that it would be even harder on her. By the day's end, he hoped she'd be picking up her duffel bag and leaving for good. Who'd want to spend time with someone who pretended you didn't exist?

Bundy stayed in his room all morning. He read a few comic books. He started a letter to his grandfather but didn't get any farther than "Dear Grandpa, How are you?" before putting the pencil down.

This must be what it's like to be in jail, he

thought. *Wish I had a tree outside my window so I could escape.*

All of a sudden, he heard a familiar sound coming from the backyard.

Thud. Thud. Thud.

He peered out the window.

There was Mary, holding a soccer ball. As Bundy watched, she tossed the ball into the air. She bounced it straight up off one knee, then the other, then back to the first.

The ball dropped to the ground, and she started to dribble. She dodged imaginary opponents with quick moves. Finally, she sent the ball soaring into a small net she must have brought with her. She retrieved the ball and started back the other way.

Bundy couldn't believe it. Mary was a soccer player—and from what he could see, a pretty good one.

It doesn't matter, Bundy thought as he followed her every move. *She's a baby-sitter. That makes her the enemy.*

Still, Bundy found a stream of questions cramming his brain. *Where had Mary learned to play soccer? Had she been playing a long time? Did she play on a team? What did she know about block tackling?*

He pushed them all aside as best he could, but still the questions came.

Traitor! he yelled at his brain as he picked up another comic book and started to read.

Chapter 6

Half an hour later, the noises from the backyard stopped. Bundy peeked out his window and saw that the yard was empty. He decided to make a break for it.

He picked up his soccer ball and slowly opened his bedroom door. It gave a squeak, and he froze. But the house was silent.

Bundy tiptoed down the stairs, then peered into the kitchen. Mary was nowhere in sight.

Huh, he thought as he hurried out the door to the backyard. *Some baby-sitter she is!*

He put the ball on the ground and scanned

the windows of the house. *She'll probably hear me dribbling and come running out, wanting to be my best friend.*

He gave the ball a few taps, then glanced at the door. It didn't open.

Man, he thought as he dribbled the ball across the lawn, *she wouldn't know if I was up in my room, or down in the basement, or even three houses away!* For some reason, that made him mad. He pulled his foot back and gave the ball a vicious kick.

Crash!

The ball smashed through a garage window!

Mary was there in seconds flat.

"What happened?" she asked, staring at the shattered glass.

"I—I kicked the ball through the window," Bundy muttered.

Mary looked like she was about to say something. Instead, she went into the kitchen and came out wearing a pair of rubber gloves. Then she disappeared into the garage.

Moments later, Bundy heard the sounds of glass being swept up.

Get in there and help! his brain scolded him.

But Bundy's feet didn't move. Not even when Mary started knocking the broken glass out of the window did he offer to lend a hand. Instead, he turned around and went back into the house.

Bundy couldn't wait to leave for his soccer game that afternoon. Mary was watering the flowers around the house when he banged out the kitchen door.

"Need a ride?" she asked.

"I'm walking with Dewey." Bundy waited for her to say something more—about the window, about how he'd been acting, *something.*

But she just nodded and went back to watering the flowers. Bundy stared at her back for a moment, then headed down the driveway.

When he picked up Dewey, he was in a bad

mood. Dewey asked him what was wrong. But Bundy couldn't tell Dewey without telling him about the baby-sitter, too. And he wasn't ready to do that.

By the time warm-ups were over and the game against the Rangers was under way, Bundy's mood was pure black.

"Come on, Brant," he snapped after the fullback missed a tackle. "You've got to help Bucky protect that goal!"

A minute later, he yelled at Amanda Caler for a bad kick.

But it wasn't until the Rangers scored and he threw up his hands, saying, "Oh, great, there goes the game," that Coach Bradley benched him.

"Until you cool down," the coach said sternly, "you're out."

Bundy was miserable. He'd never been taken out of a game so early before. Knowing he'd let down his coach and team didn't help.

It can't get any worse than this, Bundy thought dismally.

Then suddenly, it did.

Out of the corner of his eye, he saw a familiar figure sit down in the stands. Mary was at the game.

Chapter 7

Bundy went cold all over as he pictured what would happen when the game was over.

"Bundy," Mary would call, "I came to walk you home."

"Oh, look," the other kids would tease. "Bundy's got a baby-sitter. Bundy, make sure you hold her hand when you cross the street! Does she cut your meat up into little pieces? Will she tuck you all cozy in bed at night, too?"

Bundy groaned.

After halftime, Coach Bradley put Bundy back in the game.

As Bundy raced onto the field, he stole a glance at the stands. Mary wasn't looking at him.

The score was 1–0 in favor of the Rangers. Now the Rangers were making a threatening move upfield with short passes.

The ball bounced into Bundy's area. He, Amanda Caler, and Dewey London joined in the mad scramble for it. Two Rangers fought for control of the ball with them.

Suddenly, one of the Rangers got the ball away. She kicked it toward the 'Cats' goal. It flew toward the right side of the net. It happened so quickly, Bucky Pinter had no chance to stop it.

Goal! Rangers 2, 'Cats 0.

Usually Bundy tried to buck up his teammates when they were behind. This time, he didn't say a word as they got into position.

At the ref's whistle, Stookie Norris tapped the ball to Lou Barnes, the tall, strong striker with one paralyzed arm. Lou dribbled forward confidently, then passed back to Stookie.

Bundy raced up closer to Stookie, ready to help out. Stookie passed him the ball.

Bundy dribbled it upfield. He spotted Lou in the clear and directed a sharp kick toward him. But a Ranger stole the ball and shot past him!

Block tackle from the side flashed through Bundy's brain.

Bundy caught up to the Ranger. He got his left foot into position for the pivot, just the way he had in practice against Eddie. But when he started to swing his right foot around, he stumbled and fell.

Laughing, the Ranger continued to rush the goal. A moment later, the score had jumped to 3–0.

Bundy sat on the grass, listening to the Rangers fans cheer. Then he stood up slowly and walked back to his position.

I'll bet Mary's laughing herself silly, he thought.

The game ended a few minutes later.

Just as Bundy feared, when he had finished slapping palms with the Rangers, Mary walked toward him.

He turned beet red. But to his surprise, Mary didn't even look at him. Instead, she tapped Coach Bradley on the shoulder.

Coach Bradley broke into a huge grin when he saw her.

"Mary!" he cried, shaking her hand. He turned to Bundy. "Bundy, this is Mary. I coached her when she was in junior high. She was one of my best players. Captain of her team, to be exact."

Bundy gaped.

Mary looked at him with a twinkle in her eye. "Bundy, nice to meet you," she said evenly. "Too bad about the loss."

"Yeah." Bundy's voice was just a squeak.

"Well, it was good to see you, Coach,"

Mary said. "Now I've got to get back to my job."

"Does your job have something to do with soccer?"

Mary slid a glance at Bundy, then started walking to the parking lot. "I'm not sure yet" was all she said.

Chapter 8

Bundy walked home with Dewey as usual. Dewey was disappointed about the game and didn't say much. That was all right with Bundy. He was too busy thinking about how Mary had acted after the game—and about how *he* had acted that day.

Like a jerk was the conclusion he came to. Operation Baby-Sitter had been a stupid idea. Ignoring Mary hadn't hurt anyone but himself.

And Mary, he suddenly realized, had just been following his lead.

Coach Bradley told me to lead the team by example, Bundy mused. *Guess the same thing goes for life off the field, too – and for setting both good and bad examples.*

And what about Mary? She could have really made him squirm at the soccer field or when he'd broken the window. But she hadn't.

I wonder why she didn't, Bundy asked himself. *Because she was showing* me *a good example – how not to act like a jerk,* he answered his own question. *Boy, I really blew it.*

Bundy turned into his driveway. The garage door was open. He glanced inside, expecting to see an open hole where the window should have been.

He stopped short. There was no open hole. A gleaming new window stood in its place!

Mary came out of the house. Bundy stared at her.

"You – you fixed the window?" he asked.

She nodded. "I've broken a few windows

with soccer balls in my time. My dad taught me how to fix them." She grinned. "Maybe I'll show you what to do next time you break one."

Bundy didn't know what to say at first. Then he found the words.

"Thanks. For the window, and for—"

Mary held up a hand.

"The way I figure it," she said, "you don't want a baby-sitter. And you sure don't want your friends to find out you have one. Right?"

"You got it," Bundy admitted.

"I don't blame you," Mary said. "But I think you're stuck with me. So what do we do?"

Bundy remembered what she'd said at the soccer field about hoping her job would include soccer. A slow grin crossed his face.

"Maybe if you helped me with my block tackling," he suggested, "I could say you're my private soccer coach instead of my babysitter?"

Mary burst out laughing. "You got a deal!"

True to her word, Mary showed up the next morning ready to practice. Bundy worked hard to make up for the way he'd acted.

At first, Mary dribbled at a steady pace in a straight line, showing Bundy how to wait until the ball was away from her foot before making a move.

When Bundy was able to steal the ball almost every time, Mary started to mix up short bursts of speed with slow taps. Now Bundy had to concentrate extra hard before snaking his foot in to steal the ball.

"Keep your eye on the ball, not on me," Mary advised.

Mary's shins got some bruises, but she didn't seem to mind.

While they practiced, Mary told Bundy about her days playing for Coach Bradley.

"It didn't matter if we screwed up a play," she said, "even if it cost us the game. But if we got down on ourselves or yelled at each other, he'd let us have it. So as his team captain, I tried to have a good attitude all the time."

Bundy nodded his understanding. Silently, he vowed to never get down on his teammates or himself again.

Chapter 9

Bundy was pumped for the game against the Torpedoes. He shouted encouragement to his teammates during warm-ups.

When the whistle blew to start the game, the 'Cats roared onto the field. Bundy pounded his hands together. He'd never felt better prepared for a game.

It was the 'Cats' ball. Stookie nudged the ball out of the center circle to striker Jerry Dinh. Jerry took off like a shot.

Stookie and Lou Barnes raced downfield

parallel to him. Jerry wobbled a pass in Lou's direction. But it went behind Lou.

Amanda snared the ball moments before a Torpedo got it. She booted a strong pass straight ahead to Lou.

"Nice through pass, Amanda!" Bundy yelled.

Lou dodged one Torpedo, then was nearly trampled by two others. Dewey and Amanda raced in to help out.

The ball bounced from foot to foot, then squirted free. Dewey pounced on it and sent it sailing across the field to Jerry.

Jerry trapped it and made his move toward the Torpedo goal. The Torpedo fullbacks fought hard. Then Jerry gave the ball a short, sharp kick, and the ball swished into the net. Goal!

The Soccer 'Cats jogged back into position, shouting with joy. The game wasn't five minutes old, and already they were on the scoreboard!

But the Torpedoes exploded when play started again. Over and over they threatened at the 'Cats' goal. Finally, Lisa Gaddy booted the ball hard and high enough to clear it from in front of the net.

Stookie was there to head it to Lou.

"Excellent! That's using your head, Stookie!" Bundy yelled. "Go, Lou, go! We're right behind you!"

Lou powered his way through the first line of defense. Then he fumbled and almost lost the ball. He just managed to get a short pass off toward Bundy.

A Torpedo striker beat Bundy to it. Bundy gave chase.

Okay, this is it! he said to himself. *Put all that practice to work!*

He drew alongside the Torpedo, then got just a little ahead of him. Keeping his eye glued to the ball, he turned his body sideways and reached his foot in.

But he had mistimed the play. Instead of foot meeting ball, it met the other player's foot. Both Bundy and the Torpedo went down. The Torpedo was awarded a direct free kick.

Bundy was crushed. But he stood up and shook it off as best he could.

"Okay, get ready for the kick!" he yelled to his teammates.

The Torpedo blasted the ball deep into 'Cats territory. Luckily, Alan Minter controlled it and sent it flying back in the opposite direction.

Stookie caught it against his chest, then passed it to Jerry.

Jerry dodged around a Torpedo halfback. The halfback ran after him. The Torpedo tried to steal the ball away, but instead of coming at Jerry from the side, he stuck his foot between Jerry's legs from behind. Jerry tripped and fell.

Pheet! The ref's whistle announced what everyone knew. The halfback had committed a serious foul.

"Direct kick!" the ref said.

Jerry jumped up. Because the foul had happened in Torpedo territory, the ball was in a good position to be kicked into the goal. Jerry just had to kick it where the goalie or his teammates weren't.

Jerry put the ball on the ground where the penalty had happened. The Torpedoes lined up to protect their goal.

Make the goal, Jerry, Bundy pleaded silently. The fans were silent, too.

Jerry connected solidly. The ball took a funny spin that caught the defense by surprise. Goal!

"Yes!" Bundy pumped his fist in the air, then joined the other 'Cats as they swarmed Jerry.

They all hurried back to their positions. When the horn honked, signaling halftime, the score was 'Cats 2, Torpedoes 0.

Chapter 10

As the 'Cats drank water and ate orange slices, Coach Bradley congratulated them.

"There's still plenty of time for them to win," he reminded them. "So stay on your toes."

The 'Cats did. Time after time, the Torpedoes threatened to score. But time after time, the 'Cats pushed them back.

The Torpedoes were determined, though. With ten minutes left to go, they finally scored against Bucky.

"That's okay—we're still up by one!" Bundy shouted to his teammates. "Let's hold 'em, hold 'em!"

The Torpedoes were pumped up after their goal. They stole the ball from the 'Cats right after the center kick. With lightning-quick passes, they moved the ball into scoring position. Then the worst thing happened. Ted Gaddy committed a foul in the penalty area. The Torpedoes were awarded a penalty kick.

As the 'Cats and Torpedoes stood back, Bucky Pinter faced off against the Torpedo kicker.

The kicker placed the ball on the ground. He stood still for a moment, then took a few steps and booted the ball hard. Bucky leaped to stop it, but he was too late.

'Cats 2, Torpedoes 2.

"That's okay—there's still time to get ahead!" Bundy shouted. The rest of the 'Cats took up the cheer.

But once again, a Torpedo got control of the ball right after the center kick. She streaked down the field toward 'Cats territory.

Oh, no, you don't, Bundy thought as he pounded after her.

He knew what he had to do—and he did it. He came alongside the striker, got one step ahead of her, and pivoted. With a flash of his foot, he snagged the ball! A moment later, it was Bundy who was racing down the field with the ball!

"Yes! Yes!" Bundy could hear Mary's voice from the stands loud and clear. Bundy passed off to Lou. Lou made a perfect pass to Stookie, who sent the ball soaring into the net for the 'Cats' third and final goal.

When the game ended a few minutes later, the 'Cats had chalked another mark in their win column.

After he slapped palms with the Torpedoes, Bundy looked for Mary. He gave her a

big thumbs-up sign. Then, without thinking, he called, "See you at home later?"

Mary nodded, grinning, then turned to talk to Coach Bradley.

"Who's that?" Dewey asked.

Bundy hesitated, but only for a moment. "Who, her?" he said. "She's my baby-sitter."

Dewey looked at Mary talking with the coach and simply said, "Cool."

That night, Bundy finished the letter he'd started to his grandfather.

Dear Grandpa,

How are you? I miss you. Guess what? I "gave the baby-sitter a chance." And you'll never believe it, but . . .

IS 61 LIBRARY

IS 61 LIBRARY

IS 61 LIBRARY